GORILLA

By Art Baltazar

SOK!

Disney PRESS

New York

Written and illustrated by Art Baltazar
Based on the concept created by Art Baltazar

Lettering by John Green, Chris Dickey, and Michael Stewart

Printed in the United States of America

First Edition

10 9 8 7 6 5 4 3 2 1

Library of Congress Catalog Card Number: 2005921321

ISBN 0-7868-4720-4

Visit www.disneybooks.com

Contents

GORILLA in Day In, Day Out

DAY IN AND DAY OUT...

SWAT!

I ANSWER THE CALL...

...TO PROTECT THE CITY FROM THE EVIL LIZARD LIZARD!

FOR I AM-- GORILLA GORILLA!

BUT SOME DAYS ARE WORSE THAN OTHERS...

OW.

HUH? HE DID IT AGAIN!

HE'S GONE!

WELL, I GUESS I'LL GO HOME AND CHECK ON MY ROOMMATE.

HEY, WHAT HAPPENED TO YOU?

AH...I SLIPPED ON A BANANA PEEL.

HMMM... THAT'S THE FIFTH BANANA PEEL HE'S SLIPPED ON THIS WEEK!

THAT'S THE SAME NUMBER OF TIMES I FOUGHT LIZARD LIZARD! I WONDER...

COULD MY ROOMMATE SECRETLY BE THE EVIL LIZARD LIZARD?

HEY, DO WE HAVE ANY MORE CHIPS?

BURP!

CHIPS

NAH, IT'S IMPOSSIBLE!

THE END

GORILLA in THE ORIGIN

YEARS AGO, THE CITY WAS BEING INVADED BY ALIENS...

...UNTIL OUR HERO, **GORILLA GORILLA,** CHASED THEM AWAY!

STOMP

STOMP

THE PRESIDENT AWARDED GORILLA WITH A TV REMOTE, A CELL PHONE, AND AN APARTMENT.

WHERE HE LIVES WITH HIS ROOMMATE, LIZARD...

HEY, ARE WE ALL OUT OF **PIE?**

YUP.

MUST... HAVE... **PIE!**

I'LL BE RIGHT BACK!

MINUTES LATER...
THE CITY'S PIE FACTORY IS UNDER ATTACK BY THE GIANT, EVIL **LIZARD LIZARD!**

OH, NO! THAT'S WHERE LIZARD WAS GOING!

PIES

LEAP!

TIME TO GO INTO **ACTION!**

HEY, YOU EVIL LIZARD LIZARD!

STOMP

STOMP

STOMP

STOMP

STOMP

PIE FACTORY

THAT'S NO WAY TO **TREAT DESSERT!**

BAM

FIGHT

SOCK

PUNCH

LATER...

MMM... BANANA CRÈME! MY **FAVORITE!**

GEE, I HOPE LIZARD MADE IT HOME OK!

THE END!

7

GORILLA in ALIEN SPLIT

MMM... I SURE LOVE BANANA SPLITS!

ME TOO! ESPECIALLY THE BANANA PART!

GULP GULP GULP

YOW! BRAIN FREEZE!

NOT... NOW!

NO!... NO!... GOTTA GET SOME FRESH... AIR!

ALL RIGHT, MAN. CALL IF YOU'RE RUNNING LATE...

...SO I CAN RECORD TONIGHT'S EPISODE OF **MONSTER MANIA!**

BOOM!

OH, NO! **LIZARD LIZARD'S** ON THE LOOSE!

TIME TO SET THE VCR--

THE END!

GORILLA in Iguana Go Home!

OH, BOY! I SURE LOVE THE ZOO!

YEAH, MAN! THAT MONKEY HOUSE WAS AWESOME!

ATTENTION GUESTS! A DANGEROUS REPTILE HAS ESCAPED FROM THE REPTILE HOUSE!

DANGEROUS REPTILE?! WHERE? WHERE?

NET!

CATCH!

TOSS!

HEY! WAIT A MINUTE! THERE'S BEEN A MISTAKE! LET ME OUTTA HERE!

NO...NO...MUST REMAIN...CALM...

GORILLA IN TELL THE TOOTH!

WHAT THE--?

RING RING RING

THE HOT LINE!

YES, MR. PRESIDENT! THE EVIL LIZARD LIZARD, SCREAMING IN THE MIDDLE OF THE CITY?

TIME FOR GORILLA GORILLA TO GET INTO ACTION!

SHATTER SHATTER

HEY! WHAT'S THE BIG IDEA?!

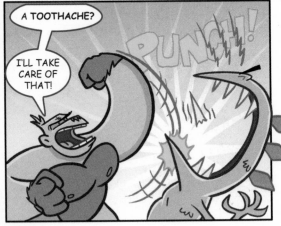

A TOOTHACHE?

I'LL TAKE CARE OF THAT!

PUNCH!!!

...AND THAT WAS THE SCENE TODAY...

...GORILLA GORILLA DELIVERED ONE GOOD PUNCH...

...KNOCKING OUT THE EVIL MONSTER'S TOOTH...

...AND THE SCREAMING THAT WAS CAUSING HAVOC HAS STOPPED!

...AND NOW A FEW WORDS FROM OUR SPONSORS...

WOW! WHAT A FIGHT!

YEAH!

HEY, DO YOU KNOW ANYTHING ABOUT THE **TOOTH FAIRY?**

WELL, WHEN YOU LOSE A **TOOTH,** YOU PUT IT UNDER YOUR **PILLOW...**

...AND THE TOOTH FAIRY LEAVES **MONEY** IN ITS PLACE.

WOW! REAL MONEY?! LIKE, TO **BUY** STUFF WITH?!

YEP.

HEY, WAITER! WHERE'S MY BURGER?

UM...THAT'S OK. NO HURRY.

THREE DAYS LATER...

HEY, MAN! I GOT IT! **I GOT IT!**

THE NEW ISSUE OF **LOBSTER LIZARD**, AND IT'S AWESOME!

REALLY? DOESN'T HE FIGHT THE **SAMURAI GORILLA** IN THIS ONE?

YEAH, MAN!

OOOHH! LEMME SEE LEMME SEE!

COOL, HUH?

WAIT A MINUTE! I THOUGHT YOU DIDN'T HAVE ANY MONEY?

HOW'D YOU BUY THE COMIC?

I GOT A JOB LIKE YOU SAID.

THE END!

GORILLA in ONE GIANT STEP FOR... LIZARD KIND?

SO THERE WE WERE, FIGHTING ON THE MOON ...

LIZARD LIZARD WAS BEING HIS TYPICAL EVIL SELF.

WHAM!

GRAVITY IS AWESOME IN OUTER SPACE ...

... BUT IT MAKES CHASING EACH OTHER A LOT HARDER.

THE END

GORILLA IN THE MUD MONSTER

EARLIER ...

OH BOY! THIS CAMPING TRIP IS GOING TO BE AWESOME!

YEAH, WE COULD USE A VACATION.

AND CHECK OUT THIS BROCHURE!

LOCH NESS CAMPGROUND

FISHING, BOATING, HIKING ... AND SIGHTINGS OF THE FAMOUS LOCH NESS MONSTER! THIS PLACE HAS EVERYTHING!

DO THEY HAVE ANYWHERE TO SIT DOWN?

THIS LOOKS LIKE A GOOD SPOT TO CAMP!

WHAT DO YOU THINK, LIZARD?

SHAKE

SHAKE

RUB
RUB
RUB
RUB

WHEW!

FOOSH!

49

THE END!

GORILLA in MEGA-RILLA

LIKE ANY NORMAL DAY...

I WAS EXCHANGING BLOW AFTER BLOW WITH MY ARCH NEMESIS...

I THOUGHT **LIZARD LIZARD** HAD ME BEAT...

...UNTIL...

I MET THE REAL REAL GIANT MEGA-RILLA!

HE'S AN **EVIL SPACE ROBOT** CONTROLLED BY **EVIL SPACE ALIENS!**

MEGA-RILLA MADE THE FIRST MOVE!

IT TOOK ALL MY STRENGTH...

...TO DEFEAT THE GREAT MACHINE-BEAST!

AND FINALLY MY DAY WAS BACK TO NORMAL.

I LOVE MY JOB!

THE END!

55

GORILLA

IN "LIZARD LIZARD LIZARD LIZARD LIZARD" OR "L·5"

SO THERE WE WERE, FIGHTING ON THE OUTSKIRTS OF BIG CITY!

WHEN THE EVIL **LIZARD LIZARD** USES HIS SECRET WEAPON ...

...LIZARD SLIME!

I WAS **COVERED** WITH THE STUFF!

YUCK, I HATE IT WHEN HE SLIMES ME!

SO I THOUGHT I'D TEACH THE LIZARD A LESSON!

THAT'S WHEN THE EVIL ALIENS SHOWED UP!

FOR SOME REASON, THEY WERE **VERY** INTERESTED IN LIZARD LIZARD'S SLIME.

SWEEP SWEEP

SCOOP

"I WONDERED WHAT THEY WANTED IT FOR..."

LOOK! IT'S THE EVIL ALIEN MOTHER SHIP!

OH NO! EVIL ALIEN CLONING EXPERIMENTS!

UH-OH!

LATER...

<<BEHOLD. OUR LATEST CLONE CREATION!>>*

*TRANSLATED FROM EVIL ALIEN LANGUAGE.

<<MEET LIZARD LIZARD LIZARD LIZARD LIZARD!>>

<<GO NOW, MY SPAWNS!>>

<<DEFEAT THE ONE KNOWN AS...>>

"...GORILLA GORILLA!"

OH BOY, LIZARD. GROCERY SHOPPING WAS FUN!

YEAH, MAN. I CAN'T WAIT TO GET HOME AND MAKE THESE BANANA SPLITS!

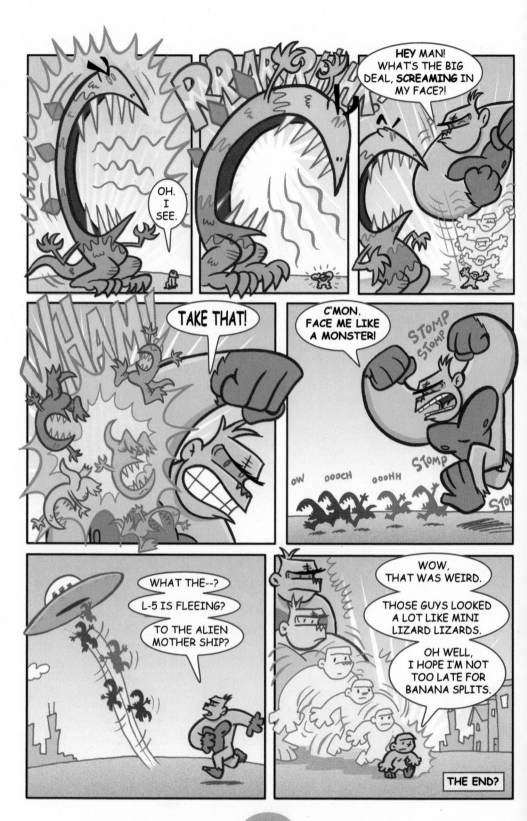

GORILLA in FREE PRIZE INSIDE!

GOOD MORNING, LIZARD.

HEY, DID YA GET THE PRIZE OUT OF THE BOX YET?

NOPE.

CRUNCH

AW, YEAH, MAN!

WHAT A COOL UFO!

TWIST TWIST

CLICK CLICK CLICK CLICK

OH, NO! IT'S FLYING OUT THE WINDOW!

CLICK CLICK CLICK

CAN'T... LOSE... CONTROL...

GOTTA...GO... GET...MY TOY!

YA! YA!

BAM!

WHAT THE--?

THE EVIL LIZARD LIZARD IS TRYING TO SWAT LIZARD'S TOY!

HEY!

PLAY WITH YOUR OWN TOYS!

THE END!

GORILLA in "THE SHOWDOWN!"
CHAPTER ONE

ALL IS PEACEFUL THIS AFTERNOON IN **BIG CITY** ...

... UNTIL ...

RRRRARGGH

RRARGHR!

HELP! SAVE US!

NO! HELP!

HELP!

MR. PRESIDENT! THE GIANT EVIL **LIZARD LIZARD** IS ... UM ... RUNNING AMUCK, SIR.

THERE'S ONLY ONE HERO WHO CAN HANDLE A MONSTER SO ... ER ... **MONSTROUS** ...

BEEP

" ... GORILLA GORILLA!!!"

RING RING RING

WHAT THE--? THE HOT LINE!

65

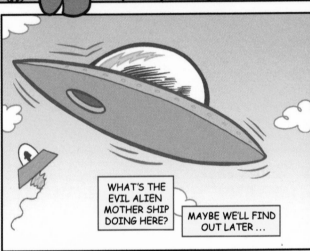

WHILE GORILLA UNWINDS AFTER BATTLING **LIZARD LIZARD** . . .

. . . THE **EVIL ALIENS** CALL A SPECIAL MEETING!

‹‹I BET YOU ARE ALL CURIOUS AS TO WHY I HAVE SUMMONED YOU HERE.››*

*TRANSLATED FROM EVIL ALIEN LANGUAGE.

‹‹I CALL UPON ALL YOUR SKILLS TO DESTROY THE ONE KNOWN AS **GORILLA GORILLA!**››

‹‹GORILLA GORILLA HAS FOILED OUR EVIL PLANS FROM THE BEGINNING . . .››

‹‹WHEN WE FIRST CAME TO THIS PLANET . . .››

‹‹ . . . WE WERE ROUNDING UP HUMAN SPECIMENS.››

«WE CAME ACROSS A STRANGE LITTLE CREATURE IN THE COLLECTION.»

«WE DIDN'T KNOW WHAT IT WAS...»

«...SO WE DID WHAT **ANY** ALIEN WOULD DO. WE POKED AND PRODDED.»

POKE POKE PROD

«THE LITTLE CREATURE DIDN'T SEEM TO LIKE IT MUCH. HE GREW REALLY BIG...»

«...AND CHASED US BACK INTO SPACE!»

«THE **PRESIDENT** REWARDED THE GORILLA WITH A CELL PHONE, AN APARTMENT, AND CABLE TV.»

«AND HE HAS **A LIZARD** FOR A ROOMMATE!»

«THE GOODY-TWO-SHOES, SILLY SIMIAN HAS DEFEATED US INDIVIDUALLY IN THE PAST...»

71

«EVIL MUD MONSTER...»

«...GORILLA GORILLA CLEANED YOUR CLOCK!»

«MEGA-RILLA...»

«...GORILLA GORILLA GAVE YOU A TECHNICAL KNOCKOUT!»

«FLOATING SHARK...»

«...GORILLA GORILLA SENT YOU SWIMMING WITH THE FISHES!»

«TORNADO...»

«...GORILLA GORILLA BLEW YOU AWAY!»

«L-5...»

«...GORILLA GORILLA GAVE YOU FIVE TIMES THE BEATING!»

«VANILLA GORILLA AND BANANA BANANA...»

«...GORILLA GORILLA GAVE YOU YOUR JUST DESSERTS!»

«BUT TOGETHER, WITH OUR COMBINED STRENGTH AND POWER...»

«...WE CAN DEFEAT GORILLA GORILLA AND **RULE THE GALAXY!**»

HA HA HA HA HA HA

UM...I DON'T REALLY WANNA RULE THE GALAXY.

I JUST WANNA BEAT UP GORILLA GORILLA!

MMMM.

<<OK. THAT'S FINE.>>

I'D LIKE TO STOMP HIM WITH MY BIG SHOE!

<<THAT CAN BE ARRANGED.>>

I WANNA THROW MUD IN HIS FACE!

<<OK.>>

RARGR!

RARRAAR RRGGRR

«HHMM ... YES.»

«LET'S PUT THE PLAN INTO ACTION!»

WHOOSH

ZZZZZZZZZ

«GO NOW MY SPAWNS!»

«FIND GORILLA GORILLA ...»

«... AND DESTROY HIM!!»

RIGHT ON, BOSS!

END, CHAPTER TWO!

THE EVIL ALIENS HAVE A TRULY EVIL PLAN FOR **GORILLA GORILLA**...

CHEW MUNCH CHEW MUNCH CRUNCH CRUNCH

DING DONG DING DONG

THE DOORBELL?

DON'T WORRY, BUDDY. I'LL GET IT.

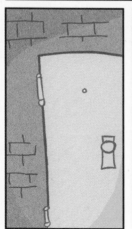

YES?

WHERE'S YOUR ROOMMATE?

UM... I'LL GET HIM. ONE SEC.

IT'S FOR YOU.

YES?

GORILLA GORILLA?

WHAT THE--?

WE'RE HERE TO SEEK REVENGE!

WHAT?!

I REMEMBER YOU GUYS. WHAT'S THE BIG IDEA RINGING MY DOORBELL?

YOU CAN'T JUST COME TO MY HOME!

WHY NOT?

YOU HAVE TO DO IT THE RIGHT WAY, LIKE, LEAVE A CLUE, OR SMASH THINGS OR SCREAM LOUD OR SOMETHING.

THEN, I SHOW UP AND TAKE YOU DOWN!

THAT TAKES **WAY** TOO LONG!

NOW HURRY UP SO WE CAN **FIGHT**!

OK.

HOLD ON.

LIZARD! I'M GOING OUT WITH...UM...SOME FRIENDS...FOR A WHILE. BE BACK LATER.

ALL RIGHT, MAN.

C'MON, GUYS. LET'S GET THIS THING OVER WITH!

IT'S TIME TO TEACH YOU GUYS A LESSON... **GORILLA GORILLA STYLE!**

GORILLA IN "THE SHOWDOWN!"
CHAPTER FOUR

GORILLA IS IN BIG TROUBLE...

...AND LIZARD CAN'T WATCH HIS FAVORITE SHOW!

DAG! WHAT'S GOING ON WITH THE TV RECEPTION?

SOMETHING MUST BE...

...INTERFERING...

ALIENS! THEY'RE ALWAYS MESSING UP THE TV.

HEY YOU EXTRATERRESTRIALS! FLY SOMEPLACE ELSE!

THAT'S RIGHT! YOU HEARD ME!

YOU OUTER SPACE FREAKS!

THIS IS A NO-FLY ZONE!

TV DOESN'T GROW ON TREES, Y'KNOW!

JUST GIVE ME A REASON AND I'LL... I'LL...I'LL...

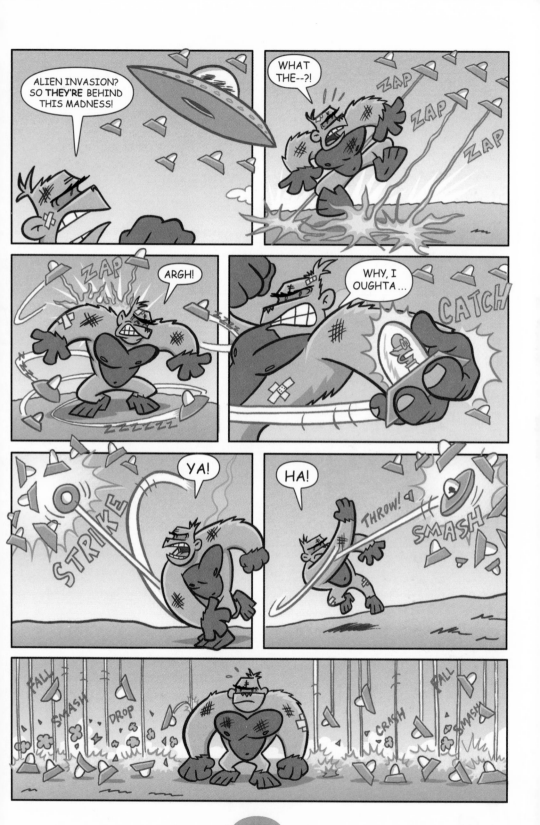

GORILLA IN TRICKY TREAT!

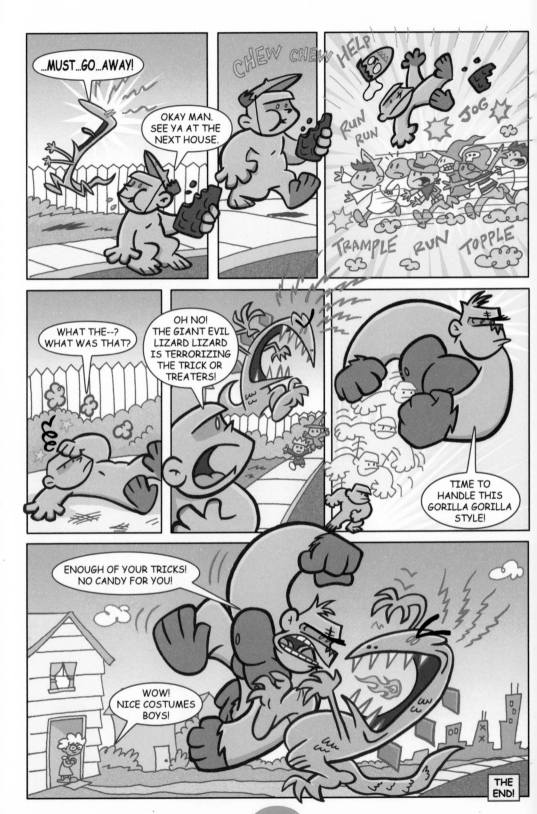

GORILLA in Laundry Day!

GORILLA

IN SUPERHERO CRAYON CATASTROPHE

HEY **GORILLA!** CHECK OUT THIS NEW BOX OF CRAYONS!

CRAYONS

COMICS

COOL. YA WANNA DRAW COMICS?

YEAH, MAN!

CRAYONS

DRAW DRAW

COLOR COLOR

SO, UH ... WHAT ARE **YOU** DRAWING?

THE ALL-NEW ADVENTURES OF MY FAVORITE CHARACTER, LOBSTER LIZARD!

COOL.

I DREW THE **SAMURAI GORILLA**.

HEY, WAIT A MINUTE. YOUR DRAWING'S **BIGGER** THAN MINE.

SO?

SAMURAI GORILLA ISN'T THAT MUCH BIGGER THAN LOBSTER LIZARD IN THE COMICS!

I'M GONNA DRAW HIM AGAIN.

THERE YOU GO.

HEY! YOU TAPED TWO PIECES OF PAPER TOGETHER!

NOW LOBSTER LIZARD'S BIGGER! THAT'S NOT FAIR!

UM ... WHAT ARE YOU DRAWING NOW?

I'M DRAWING SAMURAI GORILLA GIVING A BEAT DOWN TO LOBSTER LIZARD!

WHAT?!!

I'M GONNA DRAW LOBSTER LIZARD WHUPPIN' SOME SAMURAI GORILLA TAIL!

"GO AHEAD AND TRY! GORILLAS DON'T **HAVE** TAILS!"

NO TAIL

"WHATEVER, DUDE! YOUR GORILLA COULD **NEVER** BEAT LOBSTER LIZARD!"

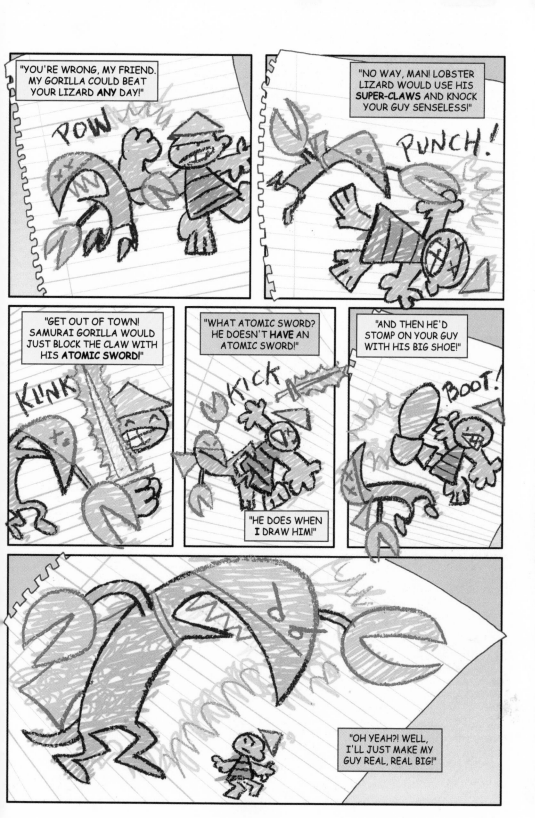

"THEN I'LL MAKE MY GUY EVEN **BIGGER!**"

UH ... AND THEN THEY FIGHT?

YEP.

I THINK WE NEED A NEW ENDING TO OUR COMIC.

YEAH. I THINK SO, TOO.

THE END!